COTTON CANDY

A Sapphic Revenge Story

DR Barnes

Copyright © 2025 DR Barnes

All rights reserved

The characters and events portrayed in this book are fictitious. Any similarity to real persons, living or dead, is coincidental and not intended by the author.

No part of this book may be reproduced, or stored in a retrieval system, or transmitted in any form or by any means, electronic, mechanical, photocopying, recording, or otherwise, without express written permission of the publisher.

ISBN: 9798288146572

Cover design by: DR Barnes
Library of Congress Control Number: 2018675309
Printed in the United States of America

AUTHOR'S NOTE

This novella is indie published and edited by the author with the help of a copy-editor. With that being said, if errors are found within the book, please email me at:

authordanceytbarnes@gmail.com

This email is also open to comments, concerns, and compliments (if I earn 'em). Enjoy!

To the girl's girls.

*"The betrayal tasted like acid on my tongue
because I knew who welded the knife,
who stabbed me in the back
and this time,
I won't dare forget why I bring men to their knees."*

SITTING UNDER A BLACK SUN - S.E. SUMPTER

PLAYLIST

1. Blame Brett - The Beaches
2. obsessed - Olivia Rodrigo
3. Invitation - Ashnikko
4. all-american bitch - Olivia Rodrigo
5. Psycho - Mia Rodriguez
6. Little Boy - Ashnikko
7. Kismet - The Beaches
8. Devil Is A Woman - Cloudy June
9. Venus in Gemini - DEZI
10. You Make Me Sick - Ashnikko
11. babydoll - Ella Boh
12. Complex - Xana
13. midnight love - girl in red
14. Just Fucking Let Me Love You - Lowen
15. so it's ur birthday - Xana

You can find the playlist on Spotify under "Cotton Candy"

CONTENTS

Title Page
Copyright
Author's note
Dedication
Epigraph
PLAYLIST
CHAPTER ONE	1
CHAPTER TWO	4
CHAPTER THREE	7
CHAPTER FOUR	15
CHAPTER FIVE	24
CHAPTER SIX	28
CHAPTER SEVEN	37
CHAPTER EIGHT	44
CHAPTER NINE	56
CHAPTER TEN	62
CHAPTER ELEVEN	72

CHAPTER TWELVE	76
CHAPTER THIRTEEN	80
CHAPTER FOURTEEN	88
Acknowledgement	99
About The Author	101
Books By This Author	103

CHAPTER ONE

Blame Brett - The Beaches

"God, yeah, Mia... just like that."

Harrison groans from under me. I stare down at him with hooded eyes, taking in his handsome face, tightened with tension. His naturally golden skin is pink at the cheeks and he catches his full bottom lip between shiny white veneers. His light brown hair is perfectly sex-tousled and damp at the temples, as if he's done any of the work tonight.

That tan six-pack flexes and releases in a steady rhythm as I ride him. My sharp red nails carve half moons into his skin while I lift myself up and push back down, taking his latex covered cock deep. He lies there, eyes squeezed shut, probably counting backward from one hundred or naming baseball players, trying not to cum. My lips plump into a smirk that he can't see. As he grabs my hips on either side and finally starts to thrust up into me, my head falls back. He's an adequate fuck when he tries.

I haven't known him for long, just nearing three

months. His traditionally handsome face and telling bio had me interested when I was feeling lonely and scrolling through a hookup app.

Harrison Compton Junior, 27. I like hot blondes and spending my asshole father's money, can I spend it on you?

The answer was yes. Yes, he could. Yes, he has been. Somewhere along the way I started to like his affection for me more than the money though. Sure, he was a little love-bomby, but I credited that to him just getting out of a long term relationship and being blinded by new pussy. Plus, it really didn't bother me. I'm generally too street smart to be fooled by a pretty face, pretty presents, and even prettier words.

My hips burn with the blooming of bruises in the shape of his fingerprints as he pants, finding release deep between my thighs, pulsing inside me as he fills up his condom. I haven't finished, but I give him a second to catch his breath. He loosens his grip and runs soft fingers lovingly up my naked torso, digits bumping over my defined oblique muscles and ticklish rib bones.

He leans up to kiss me, but I stop him, pushing on his chest until he lies back down. He stares at me with big puppy dog eyes full of wonder and lust.

"Stick out your tongue," I say, my voice sultry and demanding.

His thick, groomed brows crease. I haven't shown him this side of me yet. You have to ease in this type of man, ones with big dicks and even bigger egos, before you show your more dominant traits. He hesitates, but as I lean toward him, pushing my heavy tits closer together and dragging myself off his softening cock in a strategic way that forces another moan from his chest, he nods and finally opens his mouth.

I scoot up and straddle his face, squatting until his tongue hits me right where I want it to. I grip his tufted headboard and rock myself along his tongue, using him to get myself off. My cunt grows wetter with arousal and the saliva that pools in his mouth since I don't give him the reprieve to shut it. It doesn't take me that long - the power of the lewd act drives me quickly toward my orgasm. I cry out and shudder against him, relaxing my body until he taps my thigh, needing to breathe.

I climb down and he whispers in my ear about how *fucking hot* I am. He wraps his arms around my middle and states how he just can't believe how *lucky* he is. He runs his index finger along my left ring finger and says he could picture this *forever*.

It's all so nice. There's just one thing...
My name isn't Mia.

CHAPTER TWO

Obsessed - Olivia Rodrigo

Mia Margaret Montgomery.

Cute. The name *and* the girl. She's a natural beauty, petite and blonde. Half of her profile pictures on Facebook are her with her arms wrapped around the neck of the family golden retriever, or crooked through the elbow of her equally blonde mother. She has a few with her dad, squeezing his middle, while he beams down at her. Mia is the sweet little girl next door, if the door belonged to a ten bed, five bath mansion.

It's her public Instagram where I find the damning evidence. Apparently, Harrison's long term relationship, the one he said ended right before he met me, picked back up shortly after. There's a measly four pictures with forlorn captions in between selfies of her and Harrison, with their beautifully compatible faces squished together beaming at the camera.

There's two pictures that truly take me by surprise.

One of a gleaming oval diamond on finger; she holds her hand out, her nails baby pink and her smile wide. Her eyes are a little puffy, I'm sure she cried when he got down on his knee. The other is one finger slide away, Harrison and Mia, at their high school graduation. She has a heavy side bang and wears an unfortunate chevron print dress under her open gown. He has a boyband-inspired shag cut and is casually flipping off the camera. The caption reads, "After ten long years - FINALLY!"

I scroll and scroll and scroll until I hit the end of her profile. Nearly all of their relationship is right there in five-hundred and six pictures. He's not tagged because he "doesn't do social media"... just dating sites.

I search her name on Linked In out of curiosity and see that, despite being a rich girl, she's kept a few steady jobs over the years. She's currently a bartender at a bar called The Dutch, which is just a few blocks away from me. Weird, she doesn't strike me as the bartending type.

I take my time scrolling through individual pictures instead of just an overview. There's a ton with her family, even more with Harrison, and finally, one that shows her beaming in front of a college campus sign that reads Cummings School of Veterinary Medicine at Tufts University. That's about an hour outside of Boston. I wonder if she commutes or only works at The Dutch on weekends. That would explain Harrison's insistence on weeknight hookups.

I contemplate my next move as I idly search through several other popular social media sites for her, not finding much of anything. I end up on TikTok where she doesn't have a platform, but I sure do. I post my latest sponsored video with a few clicks, shamelessly tagging some greens company like they're responsible for my appearance and not hours of hard work under my trainer, Barb.

I do what I have to do; I always have. There was no silver spoon in my mouth, there was only one heating up my mom's next fix. She may have sold pussy to buy drugs, but I did it to get out of our mold-filled apartment with thin walls and no locks on the doors. I survive on pretty privilege, manipulation, and being constantly underestimated.

Harrison may have a thing for blondes, but Mia and I... we have nothing else in common.

CHAPTER THREE
Invitation - Ashnikko

The Dutch looks like a hole in the wall from the outside, just another bar in Boston. Inside it's nice, quaint. Matte black and deep burgundy decor with low lighting and floors that aren't sticky. Someplace for the business men to go before they trudge home to the wives they resent and the kids they regret having.

I avoid eye contact with the suits, put off by loosened ties and sweating pints - I never slummed for free. Heading straight for the bar, I find a seat with no neighbors. I drape my long black coat over the back of the barstool and cross my legs while I glance over the specials menu scrawled in chalk by the beer tap.

"What can I get for you?"

I look up into Mia's pale blue eyes. Her voice is melodic and sweet and her smile is soft. If she's wearing makeup, it's the bare minimum. You can see the slight darkening of sleepless nights under her eyes, but it takes away nothing from her beauty.

Neither does the faint crinkle of smile lines around her mouth or the smattering of freckles across her nose.

"I'll take one of those Candied Orange Negronis, please."

"You got it."

She gets to work on my drink. Equal parts gin, vermouth, and Campari, stirred with a long spoon, strained over one large chunk of ice. With delicate hands, she uses tongs to drop a shimmering piece of candied orange peel into the golden yellow drink, little sugar pieces floating around the ice. When she sets it on a black napkin embossed with the bar's logo in front of me, her diamond ring glints with the overhead lights.

"You can put that on my tab," a man's smokey voice comes from over my shoulder. I don't take my eyes off Mia as she watches him drag the bar stool out to sit next to me. Her fair brows furrow and she clears her throat.

"No, thanks." I say as I tap the blood red stiletto nail of my index finger on the marbled bar top to get Mia's attention. Ignoring the man, I hand her my black AmEx. The limit is more than the asshole seated next to me will see this year. "I buy my own drinks."

Mia turns away to bring my card over to the computer register set-up. She stares down at the card for a second, maybe wondering what I do, or why there's raised initials on the card and it's not printed with my full name. Her white t-shirt raises just enough that I can see just a peek of dimples on her lower back. Her butt is perky in dark wash jeans. She stands on her tiptoes to reach for a beer mug.

"An independent woman, huh?"

Oh, I guess he's still here. I turn only my head, not giving him any misleading ideas with my body language. I tap the heel of my ankle boot against the bottom rung of the barstool.

"Here you go, Mark." Mia says as she sets a dark beer in front of him a little harder than necessary. Foam sloshes over the rim and he lays his arm right in the puddle.

I look over at Mark with disinterest. He's probably mid-forties with mousy brown hair that's graying at the temples, five o'clock shadow coming in right on time. Conventionally attractive, I guess, but his watch is cheap, his phone is at least two years old, and there's a faint tan line from his wedding band on his ring finger.

I meet his eyes, watery from alcohol and red from whatever pressure he's under at the office, I'm sure. I keep my face neutral, jaw hard and eyes hooded. "An expensive one."

He chuckles like I'm joking and roves his gaze down my body. "I can see that."

I pick up my drink and take a sip. Bittersweet and herby, Mark watches as I run my tongue over my top lip, collecting sugar crystals from my sticky lip gloss. "My minimum is two grand, Mark, and all that entails is a date. Add two extra if you want a handie at the end."

He looks so taken aback, I almost laugh. Mia does, though she coughs to cover it up. Regardless, I heard it. Mark did too, if the reddening of his cheeks is any indication. He wraps his hand around his beer mug and drags it to his lips.

"I, uh, I don't pay for-" he stammers, wiping off his beer mustache and cutting himself off before he can say S-E-X out loud.

"Can't afford to?" I ask, dragging the point of my nail through the sugar on the orange and placing the sweet grains directly on my tongue. He clears his throat, face morphing with embarrassment and frustration. I'm sure he wants to snap, prove me wrong, show me just how big his wallet is, but he can't, because I would tell him to put his money where his mouth is. "Or is it because your wife manages the funds and would wonder why you took out such a large amount?"

Several patrons are openly watching by now, Mia is as well. She stands a little further down the bar, leaning on one hip while wiping the same spot over and over with her white rag. Mark sputters to come up with something, anything, but nothing happens other than him gaping like a fish. He throws a crumpled ten down and leaves his bar stool spinning with a half-full beer still sweating on the counter.

"Say hi to Lola for me, Mark." Mia calls.

I smile into the final dregs of my drink as people laugh before the door slams. When I set down the glass, she's back in front of me, already mixing another. I watch her hands as she pours, not using a jigger or anything, just eyeballing the ratios. Her ballet pink fingernail polish is slightly chipped and she wears two rings other than her engagement ring - a class ring and a simple silver band.

"This one's on me," her sweet voice says as she sets it down in front of me. "That was really cool of you, Mark's a twat."

I meet her eyes as I take a long swallow of the drink, waiting until the liquid burns down my throat before responding. "That he is."

"I hate a cheater," she says, quietly, but with enough venom that I wonder if she knows what Harrison gets up to in his free time.

"Hey," another male voice says next to me. This guy is young and dressed better than Mark, but he's identically unwelcome. The glare I give him doesn't deter him in the slightest. "What's your name?"

I look up at Mia and she's already looking at me. I

give her the smallest lift of my lips before I turn my upper body toward the younger man. Leaning in enough to know that the V of my dress now shows off my ample cleavage, his eyes immediately drop.

"Two-fifty," I say, my voice saccharine and fake. Black eyebrows scrunch together in confusion, so I answer his unspoken question before it fully registers to him to ask it. "It's two hundred and fifty dollars to know my name."

The puppy tucks his tail between his legs and walks back to the table of guys who have got to be interns somewhere around here, they barely look like they're out of college. Mia giggles and my attention becomes hers once again.

"You certainly get all the guys in a huff, don't you?"

Her plump lips break apart revealing a beautiful smile, one that makes me want to smile back even though I don't. She runs that same white rag over the bar in front of me, giving her a reason to stay standing in front of me. When my phone chimes and I see Harrison's name pop up on my screen, I hit ignore. I wouldn't want to ruin my fun so early.

"I don't see why," I reply.

"Are you kidding? You're stunning!" she says, so sweet, as her blue eyes scan my face and what she can see of my top half. I know that I'm beautiful, that's why I do what I do. I was blessed with a pretty face and a buxom body. Big tits, tight ass, long legs.

It's what I've built my life on, but I like hearing it from her. "These guys don't know what to do with someone like you in here."

"You think they'd be used to it with you here though." I say. Boldly flirting, even though she was genuinely just complimenting me. Her cheeks pink prettily and she bites into her lip with a scoff.

"Please be for real." She laughs it off, but I mean it. She's the type of pretty that gets you places. The down to earth best friend. The girl your family loves. The kind you marry and knock up over and over again with precious blonde babies.

"He's lucky," I say, tapping my red nail on her ring as she leans against the counter top.

She looks down at the diamond on her finger, saying so many things with the pause between my compliment and her acceptance. I think she knows, maybe not about me, but definitely about Harrison. I'm just about to tell her I'm ready to close out, recon done for the day, when someone walks to the other side of the bar and Mia goes to help them.

I pick up my phone and see that besides a missed call from Harrison, there's also a missed Snap. I open it and find a picture of him, his meticulously maintained body laid across his white comforter with a hand down his pants.

"Miss you, baby."

I roll my eyes, but open the app and send him one back. Sultry eyes and pouty lips and displayed cleavage. I wonder if he'll recognize where I am.

I wave to Mia when I catch her attention. The bar is starting to get more and more crowded as people get off from the surrounding businesses. I fend off two more eager men before I let her know I'm ready to close out. She smirks as she hands me my receipt and a pen, and squints as she tries to make out my signature.

"What was your name?" she asks as I hand it back to her, not letting go when she tugs.

I lean forward, looking her right in the eye as I whisper, "Two-fifty, Mia."

CHAPTER FOUR

all-american bitch - Olivia Rodrigo

"Hey, beautiful."

Harrison stands in the open doorway of his expensive apartment. His broad shoulders take up much of the space and he slowly leans against the frame and crosses his arms over his bare chest. He's hot and he knows it. I don't fault him for it, I don't even fault him for using it to his advantage.

I do fault him for being a prick.

I may have been born with a fucked up moral compass, but I know a good person when I see them. Mia is good, far too good for him.

I don't really know what I set out to do going to the bar a few days ago, but now I think I want to help her realize her fiancé is shit.

I duck under his arm and into his condo. I've been here enough that I know to kick my heels off at the door. One makes a soft thud as it falls over, exposing the red bottom, scuffed from walking the sidewalks of the city. I set my black handbag on the entry table next to his haphazardly strewn wallet and keys.

I head toward his kitchen, French manicured toes pressing into the expensive rug that runs the length of the hallway. I can hear him shut the door and follow behind me. I don't wait for him, just move into the shiny, rarely used kitchen. Grabbing two glasses from a display rack, I hear the familiar jingle of the sports channel come on in the living room.

It could almost seem comfortable and relationship-adjacent if I didn't know the only reason I was here was because it was a Monday. It was a weekday and his fiancé was back at her apartment in Medford where she went to school. It was a day he could pretend he had a completely different life.

"Babe, can you make me a seltzer? No drinks tonight, I have a big meeting in the morning."

If I wasn't already planning on doing that, I would have laughed out loud. I don't know when he got so comfortable to ask me to play wifey. Maybe he gets used to it on the weekends.

I fill two glasses halfway with ice and add lime juice to both. I crack open a can of barely flavored seltzer water, the faint scent of cherries wafting from the open container. Then I crush a ten milligram Ambien and scrape the dust into the glass meant for him.

-

I sat through forty minutes of monotonous commentary about basketball while derailing advances from Harrison as I waited for the sleeping medicine to kick in. He rubbed my feet thinking it would get me naked and kept repeating "sorry" every time he yawned. Finally, I can enter his room while he snores from his position on the couch

His room is big, clean, and well decorated. I know a housekeeper and his mother had something to do with those last two. The only messy thing I can see is a pile of dirty clothes next to the hamper and a slept-in bed. I slowly walk around the perimeter, trying to see things I haven't before. Evidence of Mia or even another woman.

His walls are bare of anything personal. There's two large, boring minimalist art prints in gold frames and some floating shelves with classic novels on them. I touch a dusty copy of The Great Gatsby, pulling it off the shelf and opening it. The spine cracks from being long neglected, an unappreciated first edition. I sigh as I place it back in its spot and keep walking.

The top drawer of his dresser holds a variety of t-shirts, but no secrets. The next is full of underwear on one side and socks on the other. Boxer briefs in neutral black, white, and grey. Socks, all black, all neatly in rows, folded together by someone meticulous. I'm about to close it and move to the bottom drawer, but something red catches my eye. I scoot the row of ankle socks forward and pull out a pair of lacy red panties.

I hum and toss them on the white comforter. There's nothing of interest in the rest of his drawers. There's weed, condoms, and a few loose charging cords in one nightstand. When I move to the other side of his California king and look into the nightstand, I find things that are decidedly more feminine. Lavender scented hand cream, chapstick, a picture frame turned face down. It's a picture of Harrison and Mia, like I knew it would be. I wonder if I had just missed it before, or if Harrison is devious enough to hide it every time.

It's similar to the photo that I first saw on Mia's Instagram, the one they must have taken right after the proposal. This one is more candid, not the very moment he dropped to one knee, or when she said yes, or when they stood up to pose for the camera. Mia has one hand held up and one clapped over her mouth, Harrison stands slightly off balance, like he was in the process of standing up. There's something disturbing about it. Like staring into someone's window while you drive past, catching just a glimpse into a life, just enough to let your imagination fill in blanks.

Anyone could see this picture and set the scene, but no one would ever know that they had just been broken up. That the doting, proposing man had a penchant for sleeping with other women. That the excited new fiancée was questioning everything. I toss the frame on the bed next to the red panties.

The hinges on his closet door squeal loud enough that I pause, listening for sounds of him stirring from the living room. Harrison lets out a confirming snore, letting me know the coast continues to be clear. I step inside the well organized walk-in closet. On the hanging side, his collection of button-downs are pressed and satisfyingly ROYGBIV. His suits hang in dry cleaning bags that crinkle as my hand brushes over them. His shoes are all neatly displayed on a wall of shelves, shiny dress shoes at the bottom and boxes of expensive sneakers along the top.

On the last wall, there's a shorter bar where his jeans and jackets hang with shelves over it. I start pulling down bins that rest there, exploring the contents. Neatly rolled ties in one. A mask and some other costume-type pieces in another. In the last one, there are pictures.

I sit down on the floor of the closet to look through them. Evidence of their long relationship sits right in front of me. So many of them in high school, where they look to be taken on a digital camera, the little date at the corner a dead giveaway. There are ones from prom where Harrison let his bowtie dangle from his neck and Mia's spray tan stained the straps of her white dress. More versions of them at graduation. They get more sparse as time goes on, when we all stopped printing out pictures since we had constant access on our phones. The most recent seem to be professional prints from a vacation someplace tropical.

I've reached the point of skimming when a small leather booklet catches my attention. I pull it out and find it full of boudoir style photos. Mia's blonde hair is curled and dripping down her arched back as she proffers her ass in red panties - red lace panties that look an awful lot like the ones currently resting on Harrison's bed.

I flip through and see her in the full red set. Her breasts, while on the smaller side, sit high in a balcony-style bra. It's slightly see through, the shape of her nipples just visible through the lace. I lick my lips as I turn to the next page where she sits on a black trunk, legs spread wide and head thrown back. Then it's a close up of her face, eyes shut and tongue out, with what looks like a drop of honey dangling from her fingertip.

I inhale deeply through my nose, surprising arousal stirring in me. With the little book gripped tightly in my hand, I exit the closet. When I breach the doorway I notice something frilly peeking out from the pile of Harrison's clothes on the floor. Leaning down, I pick up a pale pink milkmaid-style dress. There's a waft of cologne when I bring it to my face, but underneath there's a soft lingering of the perfume she must have used. Like honeysuckle and citrus, pretty and gentle like her.

The book of Mia's pictures joins the pile of evidence on the bed, but I go stand in front of the full length mirror propped in the corner of Harrison's room. I stare into my own eyes as I pull down the zipper at my side and let the dress fall from my shoulders. I wore no bra today, so my large breasts hang heavy with the loss of support. I hold them in my hand, testing their weight, thinking of just how different hers must feel. I run my hands down my abdomen, hard and toned from dedicated years of workouts. My black thong sits high on my hip bones, but with a swift tug it lands on top of the dress pooled at my feet.

The lace scratches against my skin as I pull the red panties up my thighs. The material cuts into the firm cheeks of my ass and the seam sits tight against my clit since Mia's more petite than I am, more delicate where I'm muscular, but I like the pressure of the fabric.

The pastel dress is practically indecent, my breasts spilling over the top like a heroine on the cover of a bodice ripper. It's short on me too; if I bend too far, the red panties would be visible. I prop my phone up, pressing record, and test it. I lean over, putting my weight on my hands as they sink into the plushness of Harrison's mattress. I glance over my shoulder, looking into the mirror at my ass in her panties, feeling a rush of wetness at the depravity.

I crawl onto the bed, not even really caring if I'm in

frame. Maybe I'll post this later, a raw video that my subscribers will eat up. Maybe I'll keep it just for me. Maybe I'll even send it to Harrison, a subtle threat I'm sure the nepo-baby would cry himself to sleep over.

I rest on my knees and elbows, so I can flip open the little book in front of me. I find the one I like the best, one of Mia in a position similar to the one I'm in now. Her head rests on her arm while her back is bowed beautifully, leaving her ass in the air like the curves of a cartoon heart. She stares straight into the camera, her eyes crystal blue and sultry, like they're gazing right into mine.

I slide my hand under my body, running my fingers over the tight lace. I imagine that they're on Mia, that it's her body I'm touching. It's her wetness coating my skin through the fabric. It's her whimper quietly floating down into the white comforter.

For the first time in a long time, I make myself cum with just my fingers on my clit. My sharp stiletto nails and the scratch of the lace add an edge of discomfort that propel me to keep rubbing, to fight my body for another orgasm. I pull the fluff of the short dress up so I can smell her perfume again, I want to block out the smell of Harrison on the blankets. I flip the page and find another close up of Mia's face, a little smirk on her plush lips, a smear of red lipstick at the corner of her mouth as she bites on her thumb. I cum again, my hand trapped in the too tight panties, pressing against my clit to ride out the waves of pleasure.

When I'm finished and my breathing regulates completely, I stand and re-dress. I fluff my hair in the mirror. I put everything back where I found it… even the red panties.

CHAPTER FIVE

Psycho - Mia Rodriguez

Flashes blind me as I step out of the vintage Rolls Royce Phantom. I'll never get used to the paps, I never intend to. I also just don't understand why these people insist on treating company galas like they're a red carpet event.

Inflated ego is the short answer, but I think it dives way further into their psyche than that, not that now is the time to ruminate. I roll my eyes and hear twenty more clicks. I'm sure it'll be a headline on some irrelevant internet news site soon: "Millionaire's Date Seems Unappreciative While Wearing Gucci Dress at Financial Gala" or some shit.

I tuck my manicured hand into Martin's elbow and let him lead me into the warmth inside the hotel. His salt and pepper hair rustles under a spray of hot air from the heater and the skin around his eyes crinkles when he smiles down at me. I sigh and shrug off my long faux fur coat, revealing a dress that's giving Jessica Rabbit - if she decided blondes had more fun.

Martin offers his arm again and I grip him, the feel of his tux expensive and smooth under my hand. We enter the ballroom and I smile at another photographer when they take our picture at the door.

Martin is one of my favorite clients. This is our fifth event together in as many years. He's sweet and docile, with a jovial laugh and a sadness that rests just under the surface. I'm only with him because his wife of thirty years passed on nearly a decade ago. In *this* world, feelings are weakness, so instead of enduring endless questions about when he was going to *move on*, he found me.

He never wants sex, just someone to accompany him, and I'm usually down with no hesitation. Except this time, I almost refused.

I snag a bubbling glass of champagne as a waiter in traditional black and white moves past us. The young man blushes as I wink in thanks and Martin chuckles beside me.

"Always such a flirt," he chides in jest.

"Me?" I say, holding my hand up to my chest. "Never."

He laughs and I can't help but smile with him...until I see Harrison and Mia across the large dance floor. The reason I almost stayed home.

It didn't take long for me to figure out the company

Martin worked for was Harrison's family company, Compton Financials. I initially turned Martin down so I wouldn't see Harrison and have to admit that I'm an escort, or maybe so he would have the opportunity to invite me as his guest. I'm not ashamed of what I do, but he's never asked, so I've never told. I imagined it would be better for everyone to just decline.

Until Mia.

She stands there, the antithesis of me.

Her hair shines golden under the chandelier lighting. Her softly tanned skin glows against the pearlescent pale pink of her gown. It's cut in a sweetheart shape against her smaller bust, and you can see her toned arms through the sheer long sleeves. It hugs her petite figure through her torso and falls in an A-line cut over her hips. It's simple and stunning; it suits her.

For a long while, I play my part. I snack on hors d'oeuvres and drink another glass of champagne. I dance several dances with Martin and even a few with his colleagues. I smile politely while my date moves around the party, talking to all the people he needs to so he can make the right impression.

Eventually that circulation leads us to the small group of people Harrison and Mia happen to be interacting with. The recognition plays out like poetry. Mia's face lights up while Harrison's dims dramatically. Mia does a cute little-girl dance, with shimmied shoulders and tiny little claps. Harrison's broad shoulders hunch and he shrinks into himself. Her mouth curls up into a pretty pink grin and his settles into a grim line.

Ball's in my court and his are in my purse.

CHAPTER SIX

Little Boy - Ashnikko

Harrison is lucky that Mia doesn't pick up on his surly attitude the way that I do. He sure notices her reaction to me though.

"Oh, uh, do you two know each other?" he asks Mia, the safer option.

She looks over to me, eyes shimmering with excitement, "This is the girl I told you about," she says to Harrison. "The Dutch's hottie!"

His eyebrows scrunch with confusion and Martin laughs as I feign coy. Mia smacks her fiance's shoulder with the back of her hand. "The girl who caused such an uproar at the bar a few weeks back."

Martin continues to laugh and he squeezes my hip in a comfortable, affectionate way. "That sounds like Ka-".

Harrison cuts him off before he can say my name, eyes lingering on Martin's hand at my waist before he reaches out for a shake, forcing Martin to release me. "Good to see you and your... date... but my father is waving me down. Come on, babe."

Mia's face furrows at his abrupt escape attempt. "I'm good, I can wait here."

I don't know if she misses the complete panic on his face, or is choosing to ignore it.

"But-"

"Harrison, I'd like to catch up with my new friend."

She's firm and I'm impressed. For some reason I had expected her to be as dainty as she looks, a sweet little doormat for Harrison to manipulate, but I can hear by her tone that I was mistaken. I wonder if that came after the break up or if she's always been this way.

We stand together in silence for a bit, swaying to some pop song that plays low in the background from the speakers while the band takes their break. Martin excuses himself to speak to someone else; I don't check to see who. Instead, I stop a waitress before she can pass us and grab two new flutes of champagne.

Mia takes one from me, her fingers brushing against mine in a way that feels deliberate. Our eyes meet and she gives me a grin before she places her glass on the table next to us. "I actually don't like champagne," she tells me.

"Pray tell, what does the bartender drink?"

Her giggle ripples the still air around us and I'm mesmerized. She's just so genuine. Her laugh lines deepen and there's the slightest smudge of pink lipstick on her sharp canine tooth. I watch her mouth as she leans in closer to me and replies with a conspiratorial whisper, "Whiskey."

"I love a good whiskey," I say in my own low voice.

She sighs. "Harrison doesn't like me to drink it at these events. He says it's *not ladylike*." Her tone is mocking, but her eyes look defeated.

I hold my hand out to her, and without a second of hesitation, she slides her fingers through mine and we head toward the open bar. She leans her hip against a barstool and faces me as we wait. When I look up to find Harrison's eyes on us, I give him a smirk.

"What can I get you, ladies?"

"Two *men's* whiskies, please."

I keep my face straight, but Mia doesn't. She throws her head back in laughter. Her neck elongated and elegant, I want to run my tongue down her throat and feel it vibrate with her amusement. I watch her until the bartender's voice draws my attention away.

"I'm sorry, ma'am, I don't believe I know what brand you're referring to."

"I knew that wasn't a thing," I stage-whisper to Mia, who's still giggling. "We'll each take two fingers of Macallan 12."

"I'm sorry, ma'am. We were told no top shelf liquor for the open bar."

I lean against the bar, elbows on the hard top. The young man fights his instincts, but his eyes flit down to the dip in my sequined dress anyway. I clear my throat and watch his cheeks redden as his eyes lift to find mine.

"Do you know who this is?" I ask him, tilting my head to indicate it's Mia that I'm referring to. He shakes his head, glancing toward her to figure out if he should. "This is the CEO's future daughter in law. I think we should keep her happy, no?"

With whiskeys finally in hand, Mia and I turn to face the dance floor. She opted to have hers with water instead of neat like mine, and the drink looks like honey as the light hits it. Her pink lips kiss the rim of the glass and she tilts it just enough to let the liquid coat her tongue. Her eyes flutter closed and she sighs like she's missed it. I wonder how Harrison feels okay with taking those little joys from her.

"Do you always get what you want?" Mia asks me. Her voice is full of whimsy, like she wishes she could relate. I find it almost funny knowing our differences in upbringing, but I guess a gilded cage is still a cage. Harrison's eyes find us again and I raise my copita in his direction as I finally answer.

"I do," and I will.

-

I'm surprised it takes as long as it does for Harrison to come collect his fiancée. She and I have made it through several rabbit trails of conversation at this point, from our favorite books to what we hate the most about the city. She's funny and smart and devastatingly unhappy. It's obvious to me as I watch her smile shrink the closer Harrison and his father get to us.

Martin joins us with a lovely older woman, a coworker of his with whom he's spent a lot of time on the dance floor this evening. They walk up just in time to be the ones that greet the Comptons while Mia and I stay quiet. Harrison puts a heavy arm over Mia's shoulders and stares at me. As Mia looks up at him with a placating smile, I stare right into his dead eyes.

At the sound of my name I look away from Junior and over to Senior. Martin has introduced me to the company owner, and while the despotic older gentleman stares me down like I'm a challenge he'd like to win, I simply give him a polite smile as my eyes glaze with disinterest. He reaches for my hand anyway, giving my knuckles a lingering kiss. I'll at least give him the props for not looking affronted when I pull my hand from his; he simply continues his conversation with Martin and his lady friend.

Mia leans over to me with a whisper, "Katie, huh?"

"K.T." I correct, pausing between the initials to enunciate the distinction.

Before she can respond, Harrison tugs her closer to him and says that they simply must follow his daddy to the next group. Mia gives me a small wave and moves on, allowing Harrison to take her not-quite-empty whiskey glass and set it on a passing waiter's tray. He hands her a glass of champagne instead and I feel a rage for him ignite.

The party goes on. I watch Martin and his coworker dance under the chandelier, anger burning me up like the dozens of bulbs above us. I observe Mr. Compton as he touches the lower backs and bare arms of far too many young women; I seethe with the recognition of where Harrison's bad habits have come from. I see Mia look over to me time and time again, and the upset festers until my cheeks heat and I have to excuse myself to the restroom.

I ask the attendant for a towelette, which I wet, and hold it on the back of my neck under my simple updo. I dab along my neck and the bared cleavage exposed by my neckline as I breathe deep calming breaths. I stare into my own reflection, my dark blue eyes, trying to see myself as I am now, but only able to picture the sallow, skinny girl I've tried so hard to outgrow. When I'm feeling calm enough, I text

Martin, letting him know I plan on leaving. As he responds, I push through the door that leads out into the hallway, only to find Harrison waiting for me.

I was wondering when this would happen. I've ignored the discreet buzzing of messages from him across various apps all night. I guess he's finally found the time to sneak off and corner me. I wonder which avenue of covering his ass he plans on going with.

"It's not what you think."

Wow, a classic.

"I think that your break up didn't last quite as long as you implied."

"Well, yeah, but…" he stammers and I feign disinterest, when actually, I'd really like to know his thought process. "Look, my dad wanted me to get back together with her. Images and shit. I'd much rather be here with you."

I step back when he tries to brush my shoulder. The rejection registers and a spark of the spoiled boy inside him peeks out. "Do you expect me to swoon at that? You're here with your *fiancée* and I'm supposed to, what, be waiting around for the next time you're free?"

His eyes darken just a little more.

"What *are* you doing here?"

"I'm Martin's date. I thought that was obvious."

Those dark, dark eyes look so distrustful now.

"How do you really know Mia?"

My smile only angers him more. It's so nice to see the little brat he really is come to the surface. Before I can answer, he steps closer to me, getting in my face, trying his best to intimidate me. "Don't you dare try and fuck up my life."

"Oh, Harrison," I croon, "wasn't it just two weeks ago you were drawing hearts on my skin and planning a life with me in a post orgasm haze? Doodling my name on your notebook? Asking me to go steady?"

"Please, this is my *real life*." He snaps, aiming his words like knives to hurt me. "You're nothing. You're just a whore from a hookup app."

I lick my lips and lean closer to him. His eyes take in my body, despite his indignation, because deep down he's still a fucking man. "I'm a whore with a whole lot of leverage."

"My father can make your life miserable."

"First of all, I could fuck you father in the men's bathroom within the next ten minutes and make myself your new stepmommy by next month." His head snaps back like I hit him with a physical blow. "Second of all, I've worked extremely hard to ensure that no man, woman, or animal can make my life miserable again. You do not scare me. I have been very gracious tonight given the things that I know and the way I've been treated. You'd do well to remember that, Junior."

He stares me down with wrath-reddened cheeks, and if I were a different woman, I'd be cowering, but I've seen the worst of what the world has to offer. He's lucky I'm feeling generous enough to leave him with his cock intact. In fact, I leave him with a beaming smile and one last morsel of food for thought.

"Or maybe I'll fuck your fiancée... dads are overdone."

CHAPTER SEVEN

Kismet - The Beaches

Two weeks have passed since the gala and I have received no fewer than one hundred messages from Harrison. Some in Snapchat, where they disappear, and some decidedly more incriminating ones via text message. They range in emotion from anger to regret to threatening to whining to more anger.

"I'm serious K, you better not talk to Mia again."

"I really fucked up. How can I fix this?"

"Respond to me now or I'm going to fucking come over there."

"This isn't fair. I met you when we were broken up and I just didn't think I could choose."

"QUIT FUCKING IGNORING ME."

I stopped reading after the first few days, letting them pile up like a collection. Instead, I watch Mia's stories. I enjoy a glimpse into her day-to-day. She likes to post the animals that she helps treat, sweet little fuzzy faces and pink tongues on nearly every ten-second video. More infrequently, she posts to other social media - a food picture here, a snap of her friends there. No Harrison, I notice.

My phone buzzes in my pocket as I walk down the sidewalk, but I ignore it, instead pushing through the glass door of my favorite nail salon. Bells chime as I walk in, the smell of acetone and hum of electric files filling the air. I smile at the owner's daughter, Porcha, when she greets me by name. Her glossy black hair sways, brushing her lower back, as she snags my usual blood red polish before leading me back.

"Do you think Benny would see me at that station?" I ask her, pointing a sharp nail at a set up at the furthest corner of the shop. "I'm meeting her."

"For you, of course."

***

I smile at Benny as he reaches over the small table to take and squeeze my hands. He gestures for me to sit and I do, tossing my Hermès bag to the floor by my feet before looking to my left. Mia sits there, her eyes wide with shock at seeing me sitting next to her.

"Are you stalking me?" she asks, her tone mostly playful, just an afterthought of suspicion.

"Yes." I answer, truthfully. What else can I call it? "You post a lot of stories, Mia, and I'd know this salon anywhere. Figured I needed a refill anyway."

Benny calls out to Porcha in Vietnamese and she brings a framed picture over to me. We coo over the photo of her mother and her nephew in their hometown, and I see Mia watching us curiously from the corner of her eye. We chat a little longer about how they've been while Benny places my fingers to soak. I can't help but to rub my fingers together; they're cold and feel dry even though they're under the liquid. Porcha heads to the front desk when the bell chimes and Mia meets my eye once more.

"You know them well?" she asks.

"I do. I worked here for a while when I was getting on my feet, basically a cleaning lady." I chuckle. "Now they're practically family."

Benny tuts. "She is family," he says with no doubt in his voice. I stare into his dark eyes, tracing his deep set wrinkles around like topography. "When she started to make her money, we went through a hard time. We wouldn't be open if it wasn't for her."

I roll my eyes like I always do when he brags, but it's with affection. There's so many layers to our story, like how they were the only ones who recognized my desperation and would hire me underage. How they let me sleep on the waxing chair when my mom was on a bender. How they fed me homemade food between nail appointments. Mia doesn't need my tragic backstory though. Her pink lips turn up as she tells me how nice that was, how nice I am. I don't bother to correct her.

We sit in silence for a while, listening as Benny and Mia's stylist, someone new, chat quietly back and forth, never taking their eyes off of our hands in front of them. Mia has chosen another shade of soft pink. The artist dots the center of little white daisies on her ring finger where her big diamond is noticeably missing.

"What brings you to my area?" I ask her. My voice is quiet enough, but she jumps when I speak, like she was lost in thought.

She sighs, a big sad one. "Harrison..." She pauses, looking over at me, "my fiance'. You met him at the gala. His dad's gala, I'm not sure if you knew that. He's just being weird and we got in a fight. I couldn't just sit there stewing, so I left. Started walking and eventually found this place."

I know that Harrison's apartment is equally as close as mine, in the opposite direction; the convenient proximity was part of his initial appeal. That means she walked about four blocks, which in the grand scheme of things isn't that much, but in this area of the city means just one wrong turn and you're face to face with some bad people.

"I just had to get out of there."

"Do you want to talk about it?"

She stares down at her nails, watching strokes of glossy clear coat gliding on, and it takes a little while for her to answer. "Harrison cheated on me." I hold my breath as I wait for her to continue. "It was like six months ago. She was a coworker of his... and I found out because of a mutual friend. He tried to deny it and it took weeks to get the full story. I still don't know if that's the only time it's happened."

She looks over, her blue eyes searching mine, and I want to offer her something. A reassurance, but I can't. Obviously, I can't.

"So, we broke up for a little while. Then he came back, groveling and begging me to take him back. Saying it was a mistake and we couldn't just throw away ten years. I think his dad had something to do with it. Mr. Compton has all these plans for Harrison's life and I guess I'm a part of that. Anyway, he's just been acting so shifty lately, I can't help but think he's cheating again."

"Would you care?" I ask her.

She looks taken aback - her cheeks flush and her blonde eyebrows scrunch together. She's not wearing a stitch of makeup and she's clearly been crying, but she's still glowing. Her plush lips part and my eyes trace their shape.

"Of course I would," she says, her tone harder. She doesn't exactly snap the words at me, but there's tension there and in the set of her shoulders.

"Mia, would you care that he put your relationship in jeopardy again or do you think you might actually feel some relief?"

"Relief?" she asks, incredulously. "How could I feel relief?"

"Did you feel pressure to get back together with him?"

"I-uh..." She tries to find her words again, but I get one more thought out first.

"Do you realize every time they came up to you at the gala your smile faded to nothing?"

Her stare finds mine again and this time it's like she's pleading for me to say her innermost thoughts aloud again. Because I know what she feels like. I know what it's like to want someone else to be the one to finish it, to cut the cord for you, so that you aren't the bad guy. I felt that way for years, though with my mother, it was a wish for her to disappear before I did.

"It's okay," I tell her.

Now her baby blues shine with tears and she opens her mouth to respond, but at the same time her nail artist announces she's finished and Mia's phone begins to ring. She looks down and I can tell that it's Harrison by the fallen look on her face.

"I have to go," she tells me.

I nod. "Order an Uber. This isn't the best part of town."

"It's so nice though…"

"It's just gentrified, Mia. Be safe."

She washes her hands and pays, she gives me a wave, and the bells jingle once more as she pushes open the door with a flat palm. Then she stops and turns back. I haven't taken my eyes off of her the whole time, so when her eyes meet mine, she gives me a small smile.

"Will you be at The Dutch tonight?"

"I can be."

Without another word she leaves the building and I watch as she gets into a small white car with a lit up Uber sign in the window.

Benny clears his throat and I turn to meet his knowing look. He doesn't pry, he never does. He just asks, "Your usual?"

I look down at my filed nails, bare of polish. "I want them short this time."

CHAPTER EIGHT

Devil Is A Woman - Cloudy June

The Dutch is much busier than the last time I was here. Louder and rowdier too. I'm assuming whatever game is playing on the TVs is the cause. Lucky for me, it means fewer eyes on me when I stride down the aisle of parted tables toward the blonde smiling at me from behind the bar.

Mia's wearing red lipstick today. She trails me as I walk toward her and I bite back a smile of my own. I dressed up for her. Wide legged black trousers that hug my hips and ass, a low cut vest top I reveal as I remove my coat, pointed toe shoes with crimson bottoms that match my lipstick... which matches Mia's. If our lips were to touch, no one would even know.

"You look like the gender-bent, hotter version of the dudes in here," she says once I'm close enough to hear her.

"You know you call me hot a lot for someone with a fiancé," I tell her, draping my coat and purse on the back of the barstool.

I watch her face after I say it, looking for guilt and expecting a rebuttal, especially after her confession about Harrison from earlier. I don't get either. In fact, she looks much happier than she did prior. She looks like she just received a challenge.

"Yeah, well... what can I get you?"

I glance at the specials on the chalkboard, wondering if it's her curlicue handwriting or someone else's. There's a heart beside one drink, so I choose that one.

"I'll have the Charred Grapefruit Paloma."

"Good choice," she says, turning to reach for a glass. "That's my favorite."

She grabs a gold juicer and half of a grapefruit, first using the fruit to line the rim of a highball glass, then squeezing it over a metal cup full of ice. She repeats the process with half of a lime. She eyeballs the sugar content and stirs it all with a matching golden spoon. Once she's satisfied, she pours the juice into the glass and tops it with tequila and sparkling club soda. She doesn't slide it to me yet though. Instead I watch as she takes a slice of grapefruit and shoves a skewer in it. She dunks it in my drink and holds it up before pulling out a small blowtorch.

Her pink painted finger pulls the trigger and the

grapefruit flares high with a blue-orange flame until she dunks it back into my drink to douse the flame. Balancing the skewer across the rim of the glass, the scorched grapefruit sits atop as a garnish without a drop spilled.

Her confidence is palpable when she sets the drink in front of me and she holds my eyes while I bring it to my lips to taste. It's more bitter than sweet, and I can smell the char more than I can taste it. I hate grapefruit, but I'd drink ten more just to see her smile. She tips the mixing cup up to swallow the dregs of juice. I hate grapefruit, but I'd drink it from her tongue.

***

I sip through the night, one Paloma and then another. I watch Mia work, we chat in between rushes of business men who've long since dropped their ties to the tables, untucked their shirts, and loosened their morals.

More than once I see Mia politely decline offers for shots, inquiries about her relationship status, and hands that try to linger during the exchange of money. I less than politely decline several advances myself, none quite as enthusiastic as my first visit here. In fact, Mark left after seeing me walk in.

We don't talk as much as I'd like to, but I find that I'm okay with it anyway. My eyes rarely stray from her, so I notice every time she glances at me, and every time I catch her, she smiles. It feels big. It makes me want to confess everything and that's such an unusual feeling for me.

I thought I stopped feeling guilt over my actions years ago, when self-preservation kicked in full force.

Before I know it, the bar is mostly cleared out, the game long finished and last call over. Two pretty servers move around, wiping down tables and sweeping the floors. A brooding brute of a man coaxes stragglers toward the bar to close their tabs. He ignores me until I'm the only one left.

"Alright ma'am, time to clear it out." His Boston accent is thick and his tone is no nonsense. I raise a perfectly arched eyebrow at him and drum my fingers on the bar top, expecting the click of long nails, momentarily forgetting the change.

"Ask me nicely."

His face grows splotchy-red, but before he can say anything else, Mia pops up from behind the bar and cuts in. "She's with me, Ricky."

"And we're closed."

"She's staying. Walk the girls out. Leave a little early. Enjoy your night, big guy," she coos like she's talking to a toddler.

"You're not the manager on duty tonight, Mia."

"Ricky," she says as she rounds the bar and I see her fully for the first time tonight. She reaches up to place her hand on his beefy shoulder, it's tiny compared to him. She stands up on the tip toes of her boots. Thigh high, soft leather, black boots. They end six inches before her denim skirt begins. "I didn't protest when your friend *helped you close* last weekend. I also showed you how to delete footage."

Her tone twinkles with mischief, so different from the times I've seen her with Harrison, even just her talking about him. I wonder who she is when she's out of the city, surrounded by her people and her passion. I bet she shines.

"Fuck," Ricky growls, running his hand down his face and idly scratching his russet beard. "Fine. But if anything gets fucked or goes missing, I'm gonna kick your ass."

"Your increasing desire to find a reason to assault women is concerning," Mia says, but she says it like an inside joke. Then she raises her voice, "Carley, Ava, grab your stuff!"

The younger girls waste no time, rushing to the computer to clock out. Ricky takes his time, eyeballing me as he passes, but I just meet his stare. After far too long, he opens the door for the three to exit.

"Goodnight," Mia calls in a sing-song tone.

The girls wave and Ricky flips her off through the frosted glass as he locks the door. Her laugh trills behind me and I turn and ask her, "How can I help?"

***

Louboutins are not for closing shifts. My feet are aching as I mop sticky spilled beer from under a tall table. But my cheeks are aching too, from laughing. Mia's made me laugh more in the past hour than I probably have all year with tales of her internship at a shelter and all the animals that come with it.

She swipes a hand across her forehead and looks at the clock. It's almost two in the morning, though you'd never be able to tell just by looking at her. She's thrown her blonde hair up in a messy bun, fallen tendrils framing her face. One of the spotlights over the bar shines directly on her, and then it's like she's moving on a stage, every pass of her cloth on a glass momentous.

"The floor is good now," she says, jerking her head in a gesture for me to come closer. "It's never fully unsticky under those tables anyway."

"Oh, thank God," I respond, exasperated. I roll the mop bucket over to her and throw my feet up on the barstool as she dumps it out in the back. "I'm not made for hard labor anymore."

She giggles and I call out, "So, you're not going to get into any trouble having me here, right? Ricky seems like a bit of a dick."

She pushes through the swinging door, wiping her hands on a dry rag. "He's harmless, he's just a big grumpy bear. Emphasis on the *bear.*"

Her easy laughter chimes again and my lips pull up into a grin. I watch as her index finger bumps over the bottles of liquor. Her fitted white shirt shifts over her shoulder blades like waves and again I can't seem to peel my eyes from her. Her dainty fingers wrap around the neck of a tequila bottle. When she turns she wiggles it enticingly in lieu of asking me outright and I nod. The silent communication feels far more familiar than it has any right to.

She walks around the bar and knocks my feet off the barstool. They find the floor with a dull thud and a rush of soreness as she settles into the seat next to me, pouring obscenely full shots.

We take them, no chaser. No lime, no salt. Dry like a college kid whose only goal is getting wasted. She licks her lips and gives a little cough before turning toward me and tucking the heels of her boots into the rung of my barstool, bringing our bodies closer.

Face to face she asks, "Can I ask you a personal question?"

"Maybe."

"What's the deciding factor?"

"If I can ask you one back."

"Okay," she says, "but now you have to go first."

"Okay," I mimic. I'm quiet for a beat, trying to decide how heavy the question should be. I have no desire to ask about Harrison. It feels like he has no place here. I know that she wants to escape, so that's what I want to give her, if only for a moment. "Why do you bartend when your parents are loaded?"

She snorts, like that wasn't even close to what she thought I would ask. Then she's quiet, biting her lip, taking her time to answer. "For a sense of self reliance, I guess." I wait, knowing there's more to it, watching her face shift as she finds the words. "Having rich parents opens a lot of doors, but it comes with a lot of biases too. I worked really hard to get my scholarships so I didn't have to answer to them and The Dutch was almost... a form of rebellion." She chuckles before continuing once more. "Like they would love nothing more than for me to let them open me a practice, pay for my bills until I was making good money, but it feels like cheating. So, when I was in Boston for my undergrad, some friends and I came here one night and they had a 'now hiring' sign. I started the next day. My parents hated it, they said I should only be focusing on my studies, but for once I had money in my pocket that wasn't theirs. It felt freeing."

Something on my face must scream at her in *grew up*

poor. I don't want to hate what she said, because in theory, it's honorable. I do though, I hate it, I think almost everyone who has ever had zero dollars in their pocket would.

"I know that I'm really privileged though. I have a huge safety net, but it still feels good to not need it."

I nod, but stay silent, soaking in what she said. Ruminating on how different she is from so many people whose circles I'm now powerful enough to run in.

"Are you really an escort?"

"Yes."

She takes a breath and lets it out while meeting my eye, and we're so close her breath fans over me. Grapefruit and tequila.

"Will you tell me about it?"

I pour us each another shot. Not for the fortification that alcohol always alludes to, but simply so I have something to do with my hands. I'm less generous than she is, pouring just a normal amount, which we take in stride. No coughing, just the burn.

"I grew up poor," I start and she averts her eyes, like any rich kid with a conscience would. "Actually, if we're being technical, I grew up in poverty. In Roxbury. In a one-bedroom apartment we were lucky enough to have permanently, or else I'm sure we would have been homeless. My mom's parents bought it when she was still in a good place, before she had me. She grew up kind of like you, but she didn't mind taking advantage of her parents' money."

I pause, drawing a deep breath. I don't look over at Mia because I don't want to see any type of pity on her pretty face.

"They stopped giving her money when I was a toddler. She was an addict, got in with a bad crowd and never got herself out. They thought I was a mistake so they didn't try to get me out of it either. So, things just got worse. She started *dating* this guy who ended up being a pimp and of course, she started hooking for drug money. I just survived, tried to stay out of the way, stole food, hid when she had men over. When I was fourteen I met the Bui family, they own the nail shop. They couldn't take me in, but they did their best to help. They paid me under the table and fed me. Their daughter kept me groomed. When I was sixteen I got my first offer on the street and I took it, two hundred dollars to go to a party with him to make him look good, another two hundred to fuck him. That's how it started." I take a much-needed deep breath. "It went from there. Figured out I'm pretty tech savvy and started a site. Built up a clientele. Jumped on the Only Fans train early. Got popular as an influencer. I've just always done what I had to do."

I stop talking abruptly. There's more details I could

go into, but I don't. I don't fuck for money anymore, I could tell her, but I don't. I've started a business running my own service safely, I could tell her, but I don't.

When I look up, she's staring at me, but there's no pity. In fact, she looks... proud.

"I don't think I could ever be so strong."

"It was desperation. A rat will chew through anything to survive."

"I find you fascinating."

"I find you perfect."

Our lips meet softly and unexpectedly. Nothing about our conversation was an aphrodisiac. My pitiful past and hers: trapped, both of us just wanting freedom in our own way. Finding sovereignty on the tongue of someone we shouldn't.

She cups my face and I step off my stool, barely noticing the pinch of my toes in these goddamn shoes. Her boots fall from the barstool and I push between her thighs, pressing our chests together and deepening the kiss. Smearing red lips together and caressing her tequila coated tongue with my own.

I grip her hair where it's loosened in her messy bun and fist it, making her gasp. Making her lips leave mine. I follow, blindly searching for her mouth again. When I don't find it, I open my eyes.

Mia stares at me with shock in her pretty blues. Her mouth is smudged with my lipstick, or maybe it's hers. She touches her lips so gently with pink tipped fingers. Then she stands abruptly, knocking the stool to the floor, and rushes away from me toward the dark hallway that leads to the back.

CHAPTER NINE
Venus in Gemini - DEZI

My heels click against the tile floor, echoing in the strangely quiet bar. The hallway is dark, the recessed lighting not providing much more than a dim glow. The bottom of the walls is a deep burgundy board and batten and the top is dark wallpaper. I run my finger along the textured print of black and gold vertical stripes, stopping between the doors of the bathroom. Men's on the left and women's on the right.

The office is a few feet down, I can see the metal sign on the door reading *Employees Only* from here. I pause to see if I can hear her. I don't know what I'm listening for, maybe a sob of regret or a dialed confession to her fiancé. Just when I'm about to move toward the office, I hear the faucet in the women's room turn on.

I push open the door and find Mia standing in front of one of the two sinks. The room is much brighter than the rest of the bar, white walls, white tile, white sinks with gold faucets. The stalls are the only thing that matches the rest of the bar, painted that same deep red.

It smells like diluted bleach and a mix of perfumes, and every surface is shining with a fresh clean. Mia leans with her tan hands against the porcelain countertop, staring at me in the reflection of the mirror.

"Are you okay?" I ask her. She doesn't answer, the only sounds in the room are our breathing and the soft hum of the overhead lighting. Her mirrored image just stares, her blue eyes hooded and lipstick smudged. More timid than I've felt in years, I go on. "I didn't mean to overstep."

"You didn't." She says it quickly, as she turns to face me. She doesn't move closer, just leans against the counter. "I just-"

"Haven't kissed a girl before?"

"I've never kissed anyone but Harrison."

I gape at her, shocked. Her cheeks pink and she folds her arms over her middle protectively. Twenty-seven years old and she's only kissed one person, one man. I should feel like I've taken something from her, but I don't. I feel emboldened, I want more.

"Are you upset?" I ask, taking a step toward her. Praying to whatever deity will listen that she says 'no'.

She's shaking her head no, but her response is contradictory. "Yes... no." She huffs out a laugh, unclenching her arms from her waist to pull her bun down, running her hands through her hair in frustration. "I'm not upset I kissed you." Her eyes meet mine and I'm stuck in limbo, waiting on bated breath for whatever else she has to say. "I'm upset that I'm engaged to a man who has never once made me feel like that."

Another step and I'm close enough to touch her. "Like what?" I ask, softly. Her breath skates over my lips and I breathe her in, honeysuckle and tequila.

"Electric," she breathes, "completely electric."

I touch her cheek, cupping my palm around her jaw. Her eyes flutter shut and her breasts brush against mine as she exhales deeply. Mia grips my hip and pulls me flush to her. For a long second, we stay like that, the calm before the storm.

Then her lips touch mine and all hesitation is gone.

My stomach dips as I weave my fingers in her hair, pressing her mouth harder into my own. Her answering gasp gives me the opportunity to slide my tongue past her lips and along hers. Her hands move from my hips to my ribs, leaving a tickling trail along my sensitive skin.

I pull my mouth from hers and trail open mouthed kisses down her throat. I've wanted to do this since the gala, where she looked so graceful and elegant, her long neck on display. I bite the golden skin, leaving it mottled with smears of red lipstick and shining, wet teeth marks. She moans with every nip, her hips moving, blindly seeking friction.

"Does he make you feel like this?" I ask in a whisper, as I press my knee up between her thighs. "Does he make you feel desperate?"

She licks at my lips, sloppy and dazed and so fucking hot. Through my slacks and her panties, I feel her hot cunt grinding against my thigh. I take her by the hips and press her down more, firmly, guiding her rhythmically as she sucks on my tongue.

"Does he have you writhing from just a kiss?" I ask before pulling her bottom lip between my teeth. Under her skirt I grip her ass in my hands, wishing my nails were long again, if only for the moment. I want to leave divots on her round cheeks. "Does he understand what you need?"

Her ambient sounds of pleasure increase when I slide my hand into her panties. The throb in my own underwear intensifies as I slide my middle finger through her slit, finding her hot and wet. She grinds against me, trying to guide my fingers where she wants them, I lightly glide over her clit. She jerks and whines when I give her barely more than a circle of my finger.

Her body trembles every place she touches me,

her hands strong against my shoulders where she holds on. Her breath shaky and her knees weak, she spreads her legs, once again encouraging me without words to *touch touch touch*. She lets out a frustrated groan when I continue gently spreading her sticky arousal over her folds, never dipping inside, never pressing down on her clit.

"Does he give you what you need?" I ask her and she buries her head in my neck. "Does he ever *really* give you what you need ?" Her cheeks are wet, from sweat and probably tears and she leaves feather-light brushes on my lips that make me want to weep. "Can I give you what you need, Mia?"

"Please," she gasps.

I crash my mouth against hers again while I finally slip inside her. She moans as I glide against her textured walls, taking the time to gently stretch her. The heat of her could burn me and the contractions of her inner muscles make me smile against her lips. I give her a few steady pumps of my finger before I take my mouth off of hers and pull out of her.

Her eyebrows furrow when she looks at me with disbelief. I turn her around without words. We both watch in the mirror as I move her hair to the side and mark her with a lingering smudge of my lipstick. I slide her panties down and she kicks them off.

This time I watch her face as I slide inside her. Her

perfectly mussed mouth parts in an O and she flexes around my finger. I pull out and give her my middle and ring finger on the next thrust. She catches herself with her palms on the counter. I nudge her forward, forcing her to arch, her hips digging into the edge of the porcelain. With a handful of her disheveled golden blonde hair, I keep my fingers stroking deep inside her. The dirty symphony of wet pussy and cresting moans echo off the stark white tile around us. We look so good, so right in the reflection of the mirror.

She leans her head back, angling for a kiss, but I bring my free hand up between our mouths and spit first. Then I take her mouth with mine and encircle her with my arms, one hand busy between her legs and the other making soaked circles over her swollen clit, dragging an orgasm out of her.

My panties cling to my skin as I shift my feet, trying to stave the empty throbbing of my cunt while hers squeezes around my fingers. Our breathing is synced as I lay over her back, both of us fighting to return to normal. After a moment, I lift up, gently pulling my fingers from her. She stares at herself in the mirror for a beat, running her thumb over the lipstick smeared below her lip. Slowly the dazed look begins to turn to a smile and she laughs.

CHAPTER TEN
You Make Me Sick - Ashnikko

I stare up at an uncomfortably familiar building. Standing behind Mia, I wait as she types in the code to enter the lobby to Harrison's apartment, like I don't have it memorized too. I follow her through the lobby like I've never been there. I let her press the button on the elevator panel like I don't know which floor we are going to stop on.

I don't know how I let her talk me into coming with her to grab her things. I should have said no, that I needed to go home and change out of these damn shoes. Told her I had an important meeting to go to in the morning and slipped into a different cab. Kissed her and made her promise to text me tomorrow.

"Will you come with me? I don't know if I can do it alone..."

That's all it took for me to slide in beside her, kick my shoes off on the floor of a dingy cab, and kiss her until we pulled up in front of the historical brick building. All while my gut churned with unspoken confessions. Ones that will be purged in just a moment's time.

Mia unlocks the door and pushes it open quietly. My watch shines, digital numbers letting us know it's just after three in the morning, but we can hear Harrison as we step inside.

"That's it, top left - go go go!" I can see him through the serving hatch, white headphones atop his mussed chocolate-colored hair, shoulders bare. "Ah, fuck, I'm dead."

I close the door as I step in behind Mia. Harrison pulls his headphones askew, just enough to uncover one ear. He doesn't turn around and acknowledge her, just calls out, "Where have you been?"

"Work," she says back, her voice flat. She nods her head toward the kitchen, telling me to step that way, as she heads toward the bedroom.

"It's late as fuck, Mia. Way later than normal." With this he pauses the game, listening for her answer.

"I don't know what to tell you, it was busy. The game was on," she calls back, raising her voice so it'll carry.

"You're never this late," he says, suspicious. He sets the controller on the glass table, then pulls off his headphones and sets them down too. "Who were you with?"

Classic projecting. His tone makes me bristle, waiting to see what he does next before I step in.

"I was with my coworkers, Harrison."

"What are you doing?" he asks, moving quickly to the bedroom. He reaches the room and I don't know what he sees, but I can only assume it's Mia packing up her bag like she said she was going to. When she doesn't answer, he asks again, louder. "Mia, what the fuck are you doing?"

"I'm leaving, Harrison."

He sputters out a laugh, quick and barking, then he's silent. I glance around the doorway of the kitchen to find him standing with a hand on each side of the door frame. His large frame is menacing, acting as an effective block. She hasn't tried to walk out yet, but I'm worried he might not let her.

"You're leaving?" He says it like he's confused. Like they're hard words to comprehend. "What do you mean? Like for the night? Is this because we fought earlier?"

"I'm leaving *you*, Harrison. I don't know exactly what you're hiding, but I know you're hiding something, and I'm done. I'm not going to play doting housewife while you do whatever you want."

Instantly his tone softens and the gaslighting begins, "Honey… I've told you and told you, nothing is going on. I made a mistake *once* and I know that hurt you, but you can't keep bringing up the past like it's repeating itself. It's a little crazy."

My hands fist and I itch to speak up and defend her. To lay it all on the table. To tell her she's not crazy, she's right. He's a piece of shit.

But so am I.

I could have told her a hundred times by now. I'm still a scared girl, more of a coward than I realized. I thought I killed that part of me, but here we are. Here I am watching Mia be strong when I can't seem to do the same.

"Harrison, I'm leaving." She says it again. She says it firmly, with hard pauses between the words that leave no room for questions. I can imagine her staring up at him, directly in his eyes, with her pretty mouth down turned. "There's nothing you can say this time to change my mind."

Fabric swishes, then I can see her under the triangle his arm and torso make against the door frame. She stands in front of him, the look on her face exactly like I imagined. No nonsense and strong, stunning. Harrison's head shakes back and forth.

"NO," he yells, then lowers his tone, "no. Mia, come on. Me and you- we're it, we're end game. We-"

"Harrison," Mia cuts him off. "We aren't. We're nothing but pawns in your father's *game*. You deserve to play the field and I deserve to be loved." She looks at me when she says it.

"I do love you."

"I believe you love the idea of me," she says, raising soft eyes back to him. "I believe you may have actually loved me once, when we were kids, but it's not the same. Now let me go."

To my surprise, there's no additional protest from him. His shoulders sag dejectedly, but he moves and lets her walk past him, a large gray duffle bag on her shoulder. For a second, I think that's it.

No drama.

No screaming.

No messy, shitty words thrown back and forth.

Until Harrison turns around and his eyes meet mine.

***

"You." He spits, seething. His handsome face contorts with rage so quickly, I wonder what I ever saw in him. "What the *fuck* are you doing here?" He looks back at Mia, whose pretty baby blues are widened in shock at his outburst. "What has she told you?" Back to me, "What have you done?"

His posture changes when he takes a step closer to me, straightened back, broad shoulders, and menace in the clench of his fists. I don't shrink, but I feel so unnervingly less confident than I did when we stood face to face at the gala. I find Mia's eyes and know, it's because of her. I didn't know her then, when I made threats to derail his life, and now that I do, my stomach free falls at the thought of dragging her down with him. With me.

Mia lets the bag fall from her shoulder and it lands with a hollow thump on the floor by her feet. She wraps her tiny fingers around Harrison's bicep and tugs him until he reluctantly turns toward her. His big hand grips her chin, and I finally unfreeze, ready to fight if his hands turn violent.

"Let her go," I say. He doesn't listen, and he's not rough, but he turns her face this way and that. I look at her through his lens and see that even after we cleaned up before leaving The Dutch, she's noticeably disheveled. Though it's been mostly kissed off, lipstick still stains her lips and the skin around them. Her hair is ruffled from my hands. Her neck is mottled red from my mouth and teeth, a watercolor painting of lipstick and love bites and little purple blotches of a hickey forming. She jerks her chin out of his hand, cheeks bright red as she places a palm on her neck.

"You fucking did it didn't you?"

"Wha-" Mia begins to ask, but he's not talking to her. His back is to her now and he fully faces me. I know she's confused. To her knowledge, Harrison and I have only met once. We barely spoke more than an introduction. She doesn't know that we've both betrayed her body and trust.

"Fucking whore."

"Harrison! What the fuck," she cries and if she thought it was directed toward her, she's quickly corrected when he sends the framed picture on the wall next to me flying. "Oh my god, what is wrong with you?"

"I told you, you weren't going to get away with ruining my life!"

"Take some fucking accountability and grow up," I snap. "You were ruining shit perfectly fine on your own, I guess I just helped speed up the process."

"No, fuck that," he says, kicking over the planter at the entry of the living room. He walks with bare feet through the dark potting soil, dragging it through the thick, white, shag fibers of the rug. "Everything was going fine, Mia and I were back to normal."

"Yeah, normal. Cheating on her was normal, right?"

"What is going on?" Mia asks from behind me. I didn't even realize I had trailed behind Harrison, putting myself between them. Her voice wobbles like she's on the verge of tears, but I don't look back at her. I can't if I want to finally own up to my part of this whole shit show.

Harrison is still in some sort of toddler rage, throwing things around the living room and knocking stuff over. Muttering about how it's *not my fault* and *my life is over* and *what is my dad going to say* and *I can't believe she cheated.*

"Harrison was cheating on you," I say and take a fortifying breath, "with me."

Her gasp hits me like a knife to my gut.

Those blue eyes flood with tears and I reach out to her, but she jerks back. I rush to tell her, "I didn't know about you though, and I haven't slept with him since I found out."

I haven't, but that doesn't mean I'm innocent. Apparently, Harrison agrees, because right after he throws his beloved controller at the couch, he barrels over. "No, you just stalked me and figured out who she was so you could fuck with me. You crazy, obsessed cun-"

"It was never you I was obsessed with, you bratty, daddy's boy bitch."

"Shut up," Mia says. "Both of you. Shut the fuck up." Her shoulders rise with a deep inhale. Her pretty face is creased with distress and I ache to comfort her, but I don't have the right to do it. When her eyes meet mine it steals my breath. I want to beg her to forgive me and I hate this feeling. "Tell me what happened."

Harrison starts to speak, but she holds up a hand, stopping him. He pouts and we both ignore him while I tell her everything. From our first swipe to the last fuck, from my initial social media discovery to meeting her in person. I don't spare any details or spin myself in a positive light. I'm finally just honest.

When I finish, she doesn't look crushed or creeped out, as if what she heard wasn't that shocking or upsetting to her. I can almost convince myself everything will be fine.

"You're forgetting one thing." Harrison says, "When you told me you were going to fuck my fiancée."

"Is that true?"

"Yes. I told him that when he cornered me at the gala." I admit.

"So, everything that happened was just... what? Revenge?"

"No, Mia," I say just as Harrison says the opposite. He might as well be invisible, a fly on the wall, neither of us paying him any attention. My gaze finds hers, and I try to ensure that she knows I'm being sincere. "It wasn't revenge, not after I got to know you."

I can see her mind working. Her fingers fidget and her tears run over to spill down her face. I just stand there, clenched gut and teeth and hands, hoping without hope that she will understand.

"I think you should leave."

CHAPTER ELEVEN
baby doll - Ella Boh

I walk down the hallway to my apartment in bare feet with my heels in my hand, the coarse carpet against my blisters an appropriate punishment.

I let myself into my apartment. At one point in my life this felt like a miracle. A space in Back Bay, a safe place to call home, something I earned and filled with clean, expensive things, but tonight my apartment feels claustrophobic and lonely.

I push the door shut and lock it, toss my shoes in the corner, hang my purse up on its special hook, then scrub my hands down my face, tired and emotionally ragged. The neon digital numbers on my oven dance in the dark of my kitchen, letting me know it's past four in the morning. Sleep doesn't seem possible, so I start a pod on the huge espresso machine that takes up way too much space on my counter. The grind and bubble of it working echoes through my quiet apartment.

Parted curtains spill dim light across the darkened

living room floor, and I move toward the glass doors of my balcony, pushing them open further to let more in. Sometime on my journey home it began to rain, and now light patters of water hit my mosaic patio table, drenching the remains of a blunt in the ashtray. I stand there listening to the melody of the mist as it mixes with the subtle sounds of the city until my drink is finished dribbling into my cup.

With coffee in hand I step into my bedroom. It smells of my perfume, but I wish it was softer. Honeysuckle mixed in with the amber of my signature scent. I run my hand along my plush plum comforter, across the embroidered detailing, but the bed is cold and uninviting.

The bathroom light is the first one I've clicked on since walking in, but it's too bright and too revealing. There's smears of red around my own mouth. My hair is knotted, my meticulous waves flattened by Mia's eager hands. My eyes are puffy and tired and the mascara that boasts about its staying power is smudged beneath my lashline.

Usually in a disheveled state I can't help but see my younger self in the unforgiving reflection of the mirror. The years of minimal food hollowing my cheeks and tangled hair, only combed through with skinny fingers. Tonight, though, I only see the mark of a spectacular woman. One I have no right to be so interested in and covetous of, but I am nonetheless.

With a sigh I set my frosted mug on the counter with

a dull clink. I unbutton the vest top and toss it into a wicker hamper; one by one, the rest of my garments follow. I melt the makeup from my face with an oil cleanser I spent far too much on. My phone buzzing distracts me and I glance up, looking like a Salvador Dali painting. I see a notification, but I don't have the energy for social media.

The shower is steaming when I step in. The water flows through my long hair as I swallow a drink of my coffee, warming me inside out. For a long moment, I just stand there, as if under a waterfall. Hot rivulets sluice over my stiff muscles and full curves. Drops from the shower bounce and ripple in the milky coffee and blur my vision, or maybe it's tears? Either way, my eyes sting.

When I was a kid, during the rare times I got a hot shower, I'd stand there just like this, my eyes squeezed tight until I was dizzy and swaying, barely catching myself before falling against cold tiles. I place my empty cup out of the shower and try it, seeking a familiar feeling, hoping to shed this foreign contrition. Closing my eyes, I let the water sheath my face and ears, drowning out the world.

Instead of the feeling of heady imbalance, there's a pounding guilt. Mental snapshots of Mia. Mia dancing with Harrison, Mia mixing a drink, Mia smiling next to me at the salon. Mia, mouth parted in an 'O' in the reflection of the bar mirror.

Mia, gutted with betrayal as she told me to leave.

My eyes snap open, images dissolving like the steam of my shower. My phone rings, making me jump. The trill bouncing off the walls of my bathroom is extra loud as I turn the running water off. I dry my hand quickly and answer it, putting it on speaker when I see that it's my doorman.

"Ms. Valentine?"

"Yeah, hey Mr. Kent."

"I'm sorry to be calling you so early," he says, his deep baritone voice and sincere tone usually never fails to put me at ease. "You have someone here to see you, it seems urgent."

My gut clenches at the thought that it might be Harrison coming to argue more. I want to throw up at the idea that it could be my mother, that she finally figured out where I moved. Or maybe…

"She says her name is Mia, Mia Montgomery."

"Send her up."

CHAPTER TWELVE

Complex - Xana

After throwing on the closest pajama set I could find, one from the top of a PR package, I rush to the door where I pace, waiting for her knock. My dripping hair dampens the fabric of my top where it lies, water-darkened and tangled. I wring my hands nervously, wishing I had the time to make another coffee, just to have something to hold.

Three stern raps startle me, and I flinch despite expecting her. I watch the white painted door warily, waiting for some reason, not sure what to expect when I open it. Two more raps and I take a deep breath as I twist the knob.

Mia's hair is wet too, but she still wears the same clothes from before, so I assume hers is from the rain. Which, I now hear, is pelting the concrete floor of my balcony harder than it was before my shower. Her eyes are stern as she watches me, waiting for me to say something, invite her in or demand she go.

Instead I just push the door open wider and she

enters, her shoulder brushing my bicep harder than expected. I step back from the impact, not knowing if it was intentional or if I should expect any further blows. I wouldn't blame her for a slap across my face, but when I close the door behind us and turn to face her, she isn't even looking at me.

Her eyes search my dark apartment. I try to see it from her point of view, wondering if it screams *new money* to someone of her pedigree. It's the opposite of Harrison's place, cool whites and sleek blacks. It's the opposite of what I show the world, dark humor and dry wit. It's colorful and warm, what I wish I could be. In fact, it reminds me of her.

A velvet red couch with gold pillows. Framed artwork from local artists that are of fields of peonies and abstract people. A tall cat tree for when I'm finally brave enough to take responsibility for the life of another being.

"How did you know where I lived?" I ask her.

"You're not the only one who can find people," she says, pausing just a moment before she adds, "You lied."

I didn't... Well, I guess I did, if you're one of those people who believes omission is still a lie. I never lied about what I did, who I am at my core, the things I've done to get ahead. I never lied when I told her how I felt about her, brutal attraction and disorienting affection. I never lied about what I thought about

DR BARNES

Harrison.

I want to open my mouth and defend myself, shout how I never meant to hurt her. I want to tell her how I wish I could go back to day one and confess everything... but then we wouldn't have had the time we did.

So, that would be my first lie.

"You told him you were going to fuck me," she says, so I don't have to say anything. "You could have. I would have given you anything you asked for in that bathroom, but you didn't..." I wait while she collects herself. She walks the length of my short entryway, then stomps back toward me. "You just gave me the first orgasm I haven't given myself in *years*."

"Are you serious?"

"Dead serious." She worries her bottom lip as she looks up at me, close enough now for me to breathe her in. "You told him you were going to fuck me, so do it."

I sigh, staring down into her eyes, the beautiful blue of her irises made even more electric by the redness that rims them. Redness caused by tears that I aided in. I want nothing more than to wrap her in my arms and comfort her. Fuck her? I've been imagining it since I first saw her across that bar, but now?

"I won't take advantage of you in an emotional state, Mia." I tell her, my voice soft. Her eyes narrow as her cheeks darken - she's frustrated with my answer.

"I'm not going to tell you that I haven't had an overwhelming amount of emotions tonight. I've gone from incredibly high to incredibly low in a very short span of time. I've felt peace in my decision to leave and hurt that someone I've grown to care about was deceitful." Her throat bobs as she swallows the emotion down. "But I'm really confused, and you're the reason I'm questioning everything… from my relationship to my sexuality. I think you owe it to me."

"Mia…" I whisper. She touches my cheek, stepping in close, pressing her body flush to mine. "This seems like a really fucking bad idea."

"Let's do it anyway."

CHAPTER THIRTEEN

midnight love - girl in red

This is a bad idea.

I think it again as Mia steps up on her tiptoes to press her lush mouth against mine while my heart whispers *finally* like our lips have been apart longer than a few hours. How is this the same night as our first kiss? It feels like we've been doing this forever, for ages and eons. Like being reunited with someone your soul knows, a tie and a bond that expands the constructs of time. Something so powerful, it could only eventually be devastating.

This is a bad idea.

I think it again as I lift her up, fingers squeezing into her bare cheeks under her skirt. I make a note to thank my trainer as Mia gasps and wraps her smooth thighs around my waist. Despite our position, despite the way she grinds against me, Mia is still angry. Her hands in my wet hair fist and her teeth nip at my lips, punishing and bruising and welcome.

This is a bad idea.

I think it again as I lay her down on my comforter. She brings life to the room, where earlier it was frigid and lonely. Hell, I was despondent and cold until I met her, noticeably sad, but still radiant and hopeful. I know this is unhealthy, how big my feelings are already. How she feels like the only thing I'd need to keep going on my worst days. How bad I'll feel when she leaves, when she remembers what I did, when she realizes I'm too broken to love her correctly.

She stares up at me, hair a golden halo against the dark bedding. Before she came over, she must have scrubbed the makeup from her face, because I can count the freckles sprinkled across her nose and I can no longer see the stains of red on her mouth. Her blue eyes are wary with a glimmer of ire. She's so beautiful, I lean down and kiss her again. If this is self destruction then I'm a willing participant.

This is a bad idea.

I think it again as I throw her boots to the floor, as I pull her skirt and panties off, as I let her shirt join the pile. And again as I draw mewling moans from her when I suck her nipples into my mouth, one by one. And again as I bite the underside of her breast and tickle her ribs with my hair. And again as I smile up at her from between her thighs.

Fuck it.

I think it as I swipe my tongue through her pussy. The flavor of her sticky arousal bursts on my tongue, clean and a little salty from her orgasm at the bar. She spreads her thighs wider and I admire the petal-like folds of her labia, running a gentle finger around them, wetting it before sliding inside her.

Her back arches as I stroke deep, finding that spot at the same time I lick over her clit over and over before I suck at it, making her writhe against my comforter. I pull my finger out and rim her opening with the tip of my tongue before pushing inside of her, feeling her inner muscles contract and a gush of arousal pool in my mouth, dripping down her slit, over my chin, wetting the bed beneath her.

She cries out when I pinch her nipple between my red painted fingers, then moans when I flip her over. I position her first, propping her pliant body on hands and knees. Then I settle under her, beneath her spread thighs.

The irony of our position isn't lost on me. This is how I took back my power against Harrison when just the lone word of her name hurt me. I can admit that now, it hurt to realize I meant so little. That I was so easily replaceable.

I know it hurt her to feel the same.

She stares down at me for a beat, the curtain of her hair falls over us and I nod. I want her to be in control, I want to ignore the throb of my own cunt and give her all the pleasure she wants. I deserve that. So does she.

I open my mouth as she squats down, her pussy barely touching my outstretched tongue. I reach up and grab her by the crease of her thighs, pulling her down on my face. Cliche, but if I die, I die. Her warbled voice begging me, the last thing that I'd hear as she grinds herself down on my face, would be an excellent way to go.

My nose rubs her clit as she rocks faster and faster, moans and mewls and pretty little sobs falling from her lips as she does it. My iron headboard hits the wall, playing us a background song of filth. I grip her soft skin, holding her gently, letting her take what she needs.

"Oh god. Oh K..." she cries out as she shudders, her thighs shaking on either side of my head. She shifts so she's off of my mouth and I take a deep breath, ignoring the tingles of air deprivation as I pull her close again. Nuzzling my wet cheeks against her inner thighs, she jerks as I try to tongue her clean. She hisses through her teeth at the sensitivity.

Her panting breaths make me glow, my heart warm and my belly full of hope. My empty cunt pulses and I try to ignore it as she settles next to me. My thighs rub together as she leans forward. I part my lips, expecting her mouth on mine, but instead she runs her tongue over my skin, tasting herself on my chin, my cheeks, the corners of my lips.

I groan as her hands touch me over the thin bamboo of my pajama set. She squeezes my large breast, tiny fingers sinking deep in the soft flesh. She slowly unbuttons the top, trailing cold digits over my sternum and the muscles of my stomach, dipping into my belly button before pushing my shorts off my hips.

She watches me, eyes less angry, but still reserved. She watches every twitch she causes and every shift of breath her touch draws out of me. When she finally has mercy and slides her hand between my legs, I sigh. She gasps at how wet she finds me. I feel it slick between my lips and dripping down the crack of my ass.

Mia plays there, just touching. She gathers my wetness as she strokes around my opening. She explores my folds, which are more shallow than hers, less blossoming but so responsive. She finds my clit swollen and she touches me gently at first, then more firmly, drawing a deep moan from me which she seems to like, because she keeps that pressure as she begins to make circles.

"Mia…" I whisper her name, blindly reaching for her mouth with mine, but she doesn't let me.

"Do you know how dumb it is that I *still* don't know your name," she says, her voice delicate and venomous. My eyes remain closed, but I feel her indignation as she circles faster, as if proving a point.

My body winds up tighter and tighter and I'm dying to touch her again. Instead I keep my voice low and tell her, "Katya. My name is Katya."

She rewards me by sliding a finger inside and exploring there too, stroking the tight muscled walls and eventually the ridges of my g-spot. She adds a second finger and hums as I let an approving moan out. She finds a pace that resonates with us both and continues her ministrations, circling my clit at the same time, and suddenly I'm so close.

"More," I say, and her movements falter for a moment as she contemplates my request. She glances down where her fingers are still inside me and I watch her as she watches herself pull her fingers out before adding a third. It's not easy and she worries her bottom lip as she stretches me. When all three fingers are seated, she tries to find her rhythm again, hesitant until I lift my hips to push against her.

"You're so tight this way," she whispers. Then she commits, fingering me harder than I did her, drawing sounds from my throat that make her more confident. She shifts so she can continue fucking me, but also taste me for the first time. The tip of her tongue taps against my clit and I watch her face change from determination to pure hunger. "Oh, fuck…"

It doesn't take long after that. I quickly rush toward my orgasm and she feasts on me like she's never had anything better. Even after I convulse around her fingers and she pulls them from me, she laps at my cunt with blind adoration and fervor, until I'm nearly begging her to stop.

When she finally does, she lays her petite body over mine, tangling our tongues and mingling our flavors. We kiss until her lips puff up and mine feel bruised; our bodies intertwine and don't separate again.

Just when I think she's asleep, I hear her whisper my name. I give an answering hum, but she doesn't respond. Maybe she just wanted to see what it felt like to say it. I wonder if she likes the taste of it as much as she liked the taste of me.

For once I don't hate the sound of it. I don't think of my mother and how she said it was a family name. How I shared it with people who gave up on me long before I deserved it. I don't think of how it means "pure" and how I'm the furthest from that. I just think of how lovely it sounds in her perfect, sleepy voice and how I can coax it from her again.

***

I wake on my stomach with my face buried in my pillow that smells like honeysuckle and amber - it's a lovelier mix than I could have imagined. The sun glows so strongly through my closed eyelids, I know it has to be at least noon. I roll on my back and stretch, reaching out to feel for Mia. The other side of the bed is cold again.

She's not there.

She's not in my bathroom, living room, kitchen, or standing on my balcony.

Her clothes aren't on my floor.

She's gone.

I pick up my phone but don't find anything other than a missed message from her last night asking where I lived. I was hopeful for something that told me where we stood. My call goes straight to voicemail.

The espresso machine grinds in the kitchen, and I stand in front of the doors to my balcony, just like last night. Groundhog Day syndrome eats away at me as I anticipate a knock at the door, Mia standing there demanding my attention once again.

But she told me I owed her, and I guess it was paid in full in just one night.

CHAPTER FOURTEEN

Just Fucking Let Me Love You - Lowen

Six Weeks Later

I shouldn't go in.

I haven't been back to The Dutch since Mia ghosted me a month and a half ago. But I just finished dinner with Martin, where he told me he wouldn't be needing any dates any time soon due to his new co-worker girlfriend, and I'm feeling somewhat raw.

I don't know if stopping in a bar that simultaneously brings back equally happy and disastrous memories is rubbing salt in my own wound or a balm. It's a Wednesday so Mia should be at school, I should be safe to sit at the bar and ignore businessmen with a drink to ease my mind before I head home to my quiet apartment.

The bells above the door chime in a familiar way. The TVs keep the attention of the patrons, they chant and cheer as someone does something with some kind of ball. A waitress rushes past me with a yin and yang of empty and overflowing pitchers of beer on her tray. The big burly guy from before is behind the bar.

My sigh of relief gets caught in my throat as the two-way door to the kitchen pushes open and there stands Mia. She's cut her golden hair to her shoulders since the last time I saw her. Her white t-shirt is cropped at her belly button and the black letters that proclaim her place of employment stretch tight over her breasts. She smiles at Ricky and he scowls back.

Then her eyes meet mine and her smile doesn't quite fall, but it shifts into something hesitant. I walk down the empty stretch of floor between the tall round tables, an uncertain runway where she's my only spectator.

The seat at the bar is the same one I've sat in before and she glides over just like she always has.

"You still stalking me?" she asks, her tone not quite playful.

"It's a weekday," I reply, simply.

"Spring break," she answers my non-question. "What can I get you?"

I glance over at the chalkboard menu, her curlicue handwriting spelling out Cotton Candy Cosmo with her signature heart doodled next to it. I point and she nods, turning to gather her supplies.

She rims a thin-stemmed martini glass with pink sugar crystals and sets it to the side. In her shaker she adds vanilla vodka over ice, then triple sec, some cranberry juice, and a squeeze of lime. She eyeballs it all, too practiced to reach for any measurement apparatus.

When she turns on a cotton candy machine, I almost let out a laugh. I don't know why I would expect store-bought or anything less than her full effort. We both watch as the sugar spins, nearly invisible at first, then thin as a spider web as it comes together on the cone. Fluffy, delicate, and the same pink as Mia's fingernails.

She pours pink liquid from the shaker, and with a dash of edible glitter and a stir with her long golden spoon, it's a whirlpool of shimmering pink. Only when it's settled does she gently place the cloud of pink on top.

It instantly starts to dissolve, there's barely even a chance to admire it.

"Have you been okay?" I ask her, not looking up, just tilting the drink up. It's almost too sweet, but the hint of lime juice cuts through just enough. I lick my lips and finally meet her eyes.

"I've been really great," she says. "I've left Harrison for good. I'm letting my parents lease me a second apartment out here, not far from yours, actually. I've gone on a few dates…"

The saccharine taste in my mouth turns bitter at the idea of her dating, of anyone getting the pieces of her I want for myself. I bite my lip to distract from the jealousy I have no right feeling.

"Anyone promising?"

She shrugs. "No one has enticed me on a second date yet."

"Poor guys," I say with no conviction.

She laughs, and for a second there's no messy history between us. She shakes her head and corrects me. "Girls." I nod and give her a smile, understanding with just a word that she's found what frees her.

We make idle chit-chat between customers, but she doesn't linger like she once did, so neither do I. I finish my drink, the dregs thick with melted cotton candy. I swallow against it, or maybe against the lump in my throat. I want to ask her if she's thought about me as much as I have her. If I made the same kind of impact in her life. If she wanted to go out sometime.

Instead I close my tab with Ricky and sneak out while she's at the opposite end of the bar and take a cab back to my apartment.

I kick off my heels at the door and pour myself a glass of wine. A little meow comes from my living room and I pad over the ornate rug to see my new baby. The cat tower is no longer empty and I'm working my way toward being okay with attachment. The kitten pokes his orange head out of the top hole, eye level with me, and paws the air for my attention. I rub his head and kiss his pink nose, and he purrs so loudly I almost don't hear my phone buzzing against the kitchen counter.

Mia's contact photo stares back at me. It's a candid picture of her behind the bar that I took the night we first kissed. I open the message and see that it's just an address at first, an apartment complex the next block over.

Then my phone buzzes again and I smile, warmth spreading in my belly.

"Your place or mine?"

THE END

This epilogue is optional - it's also not your conventional Happily Ever After.

Here you'll find them happy, but in a bittersweet, realistic - things don't always work out how you want them to - way.

DR BARNES

EPILOGUE
so it's your birthday - Xana

Eight Years Later

Love is complicated. Mia and I, we were complicated. We were two young adults navigating our first real go at a love so big we didn't know what to do with it. It was passionate and toxic and perfect learning fodder. Our love was as sticky and messy and fragile as the cotton candy that covers my daughter's chubby fingers right now.

Ophelia smiles up at me, her white baby teeth on full display, the corners of her mouth stained blue. I run my hand over the top of her head, over the protective braids I learned to do just for her. On her other side my husband, Derrick, digs into a comically large turkey leg. All around are the sounds of the fair, loud and crowded and jolly clown-like jingles.

I nod toward a funnel cake line, where I see Mia standing there in a bright pink sundress. She holds the hand of a tall, tan woman, with short dark hair. I haven't seen her in years, but I'd recognize her anywhere.

We step into line behind them and I tap her shoulder. When she turns, her face lights up in a familiar way, like I'd seen it so many times before. For a second I see her younger self, behind a bar, across a ball room, staring up at me from my bed, but that was then. Now she's got soft lines around her eyes and smile lines around her mouth. She hugs me tight and she no longer smells like honeysuckle, but something smokier and more mature.

"God, has it been so long that I didn't know you had a kid?" She whispers during the embrace.

It's been six years since we parted ways for good. After two chaotic, on-again-off-again years for us, I wasn't looking for anyone. It was about six months post break up that I got a date request. It simply read, "I'm a newly single dad of a six month old. I have this stupid wedding to go to and I don't want to go alone." It was last-minute and all of my girls were booked, but despite not having worked for years, I couldn't let him down. When he opened the door, my first thought was of how handsome he was, the second was how loud his baby was. His sitter canceled, he forgot to call me, he was sleep deprived and upset. I pushed right past him and picked his little girl up. He said that was the first time since his ex left that she stopped crying... we didn't make it to that wedding.

I smile as we pull away, "I adopted her when Derrick and I got married."

"The girl who was scared to own a cat," she grins, "look at you now."

When I introduce Derrick, his deep brown skin crinkles around his beautiful, white smile. He shifts his food around to shake hands, Ophie smiles too, her dad's smile. Her eyes are her mother's, but she's long gone. An addict, like my mom, but my baby will never have to struggle like I did.

"This is Alonna," Mia says, pulling the woman a little closer, "my fiancée." She's stunning, more masc than Mia, with her pixie cut and cargo pants. They're perfect counterparts, and they beam at each other with palpable affection. "This is K.T."

The look on Alonna's face tells me that she knows who I am, just as Derrick does Mia. There's too much history not to have shared with our partners, too much of each other that made us who we are today.

Mia tells us how they met at a convention. They're both veterinarians, her household pets and Alonna's farm animals. They've been together a little over a year and just recently got engaged. They're building a house with a combined practice on their property. They're blissful, it's easy for anyone to see.

"Mama, can I go ride?" Ophie interrupts, pointing emphatically to a brightly-colored, toddler-sized roller coaster a few yards away.

I give her a nod and Derrick says his goodbyes, leading her toward a trashcan first.

"It was so good to see you, Katya."

"I'm so glad you're happy, Mia."

I catch up with my family, taking Derrick's hand on my right and Ophelia's blue fingers in the other. Glancing over my shoulder I see Mia wave and I smile, feeling thankful and content and a little sticky sweet.

ACKNOWLEDGEMENT

This book was such a fun one to write. I challenged myself to write from one POV and keep her name to the very end. I wanted to write women from the female gaze, I wanted to write something pretty and sultry. I hope I delivered!

As usual, I have to shout out my alpha-readers Tanya, Darla, Chelsea, and now Ari, who went from beta to alpha for this one because I needed endless validation. The comment crack you all provide is life-giving. Thank you to Alex and Kera for beta reading. Thank you to Taylor for being the best, most generous copy-editor-friend in the entire world.

Thank you to Olivia Rodrigo for writing 'obsessed' and inspiring this whole novella.

ABOUT THE AUTHOR

Dr Barnes

DR Barnes is a small town Texas girl who moved to Louisiana at eighteen for college and instead found love and stuck around. She is a mother of three beautiful, long-haired boys. When she's not writing, she's working as the manager of a popular retail store, reading, or chasing feral twins. She has a deep love for complicated FMCs and pining leading men. She will never stick to one genre, you can't make her. She loves coffee, painting naked ladies, and laughing at stupid videos late at night with her husband.

BOOKS BY THIS AUTHOR

Wild Thing

Appalachia taught Leah about the monsters who hide in the dark. The trouble was she was never afraid of the dark, and she craved the monsters.

Life taught Leah that the real monsters are human, and craving monsters is dangerous, so she chose to seek her thrills in other ways. That's how she finds herself locked in a dark basement alone... or so she thinks. When she begins hearing sounds like footsteps and the distant call of her name, she must decide whether to fight the fear or succumb to it. When she comes face to face - or mask - with her specter, she must decide whether to cower or play his game.

Run, Wild Thing.

Bareback

Henry Sky's first trip to the National Finals Rodeo isn't exactly going to plan. After walking in on his girlfriend with rodeo's current heartthrob and her telling the whole internet about it, he's understandably out of sorts. Uncomfortable with all the attention and lack of help from his friends, the only one who seems to know how to distract him is his stoic, mysterious roping partner...

Ansel Cartridge has been around the rodeo scene for a while and knows just how hard it is to be the center of attention. In hopes of getting Henry out of his head, Ansel opens himself up, giving Henry a glimpse into his life that no one else gets. Now if he can just keep his feelings under control...

Together they'll explore the city and themselves and figure out if what happens in Vegas has to stay in Vegas this time.

Printed in Dunstable, United Kingdom